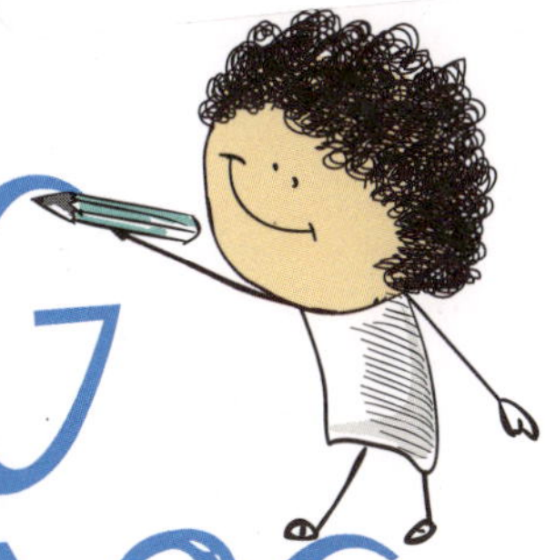

DRAWING & PAINTING TECHNIQUES

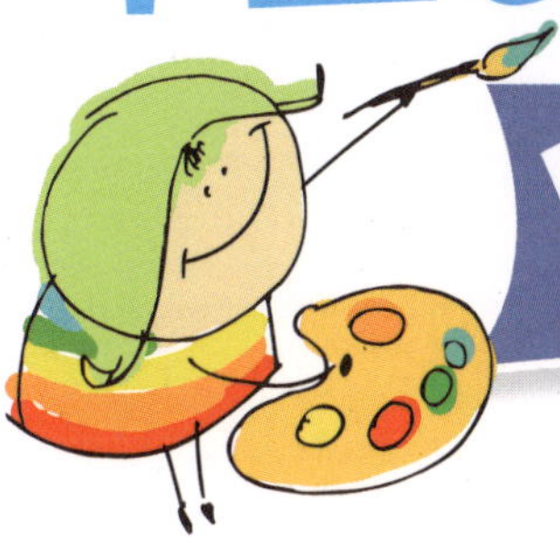

WORKBOOK

Level 1

Om KIDZ

An imprint of Om Books International

Doodle Away

Let us doodle! Trace over the faded design first. Then, fill up the rest of the box.

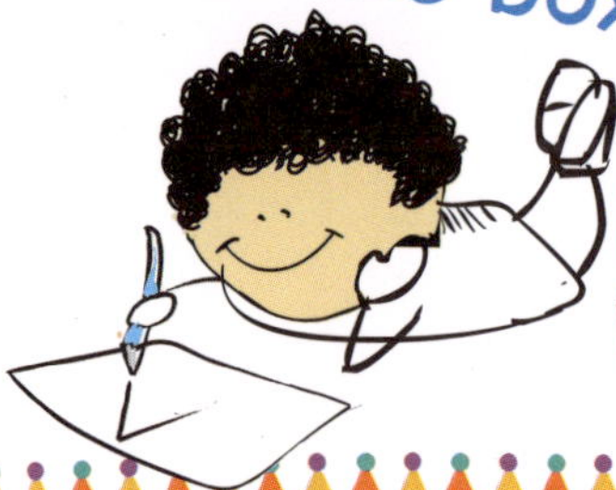

Use lines, shapes and dots to complete the doodle.

Primary Portrait

Use primary colours to make this picture colourful.

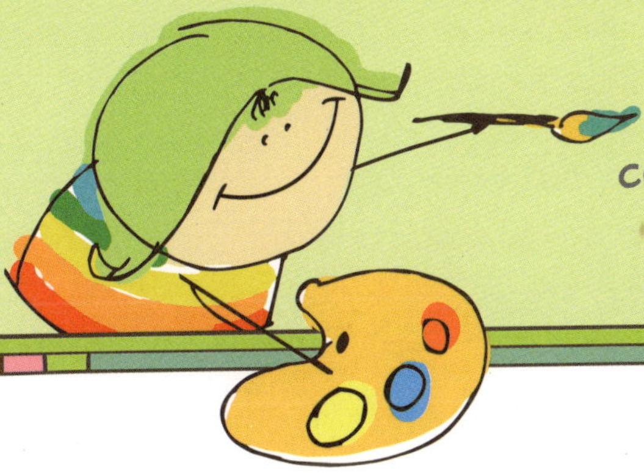

Red, blue and yellow are primary colours. When we mix them together, we get secondary colours.

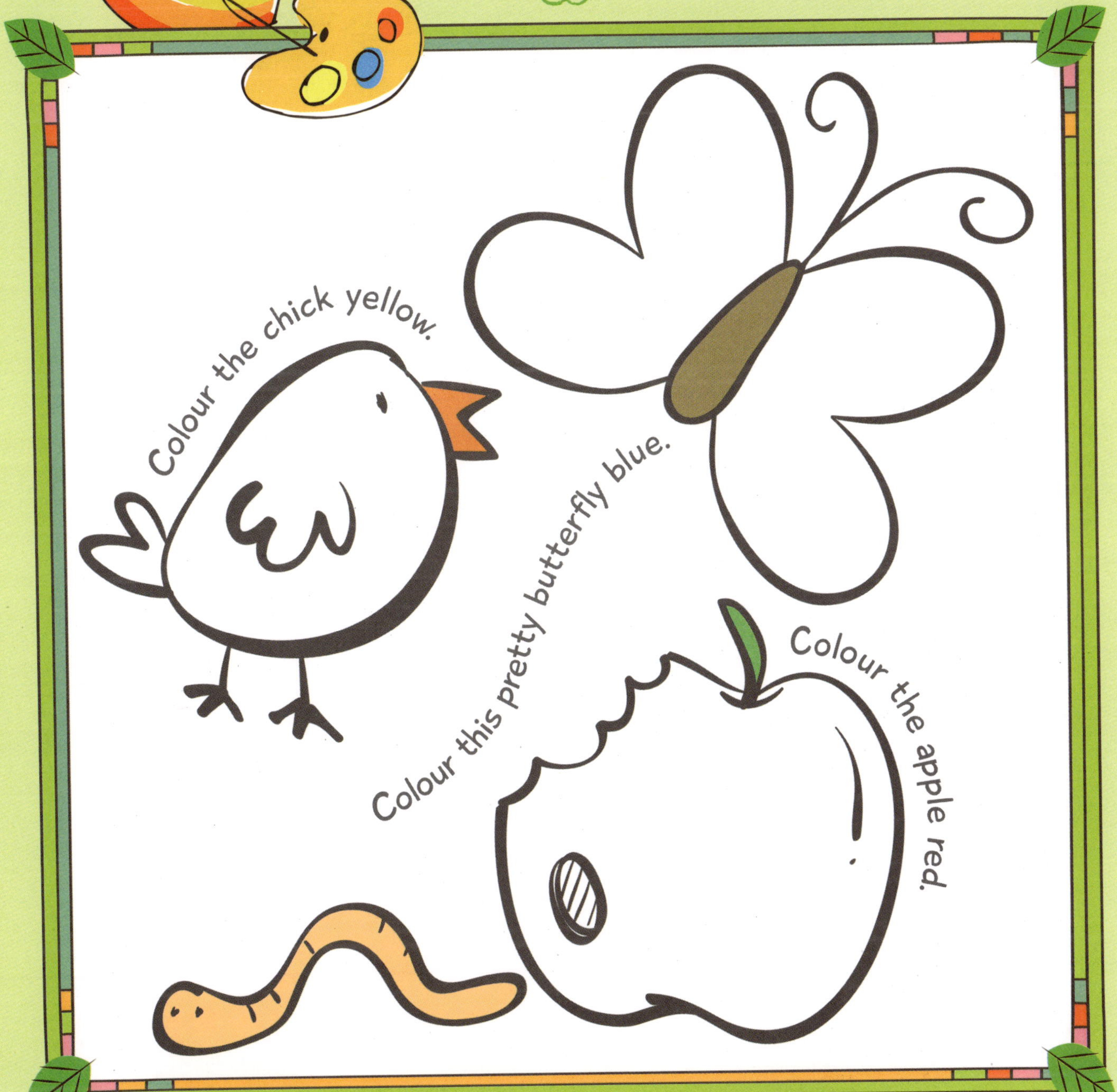

Print-a-pattern

Use your fingers to create art! Dip your index finger in paint and create a curvy pattern like the one below. Once you complete a curve, dip your finger in another colour and continue making more curves!

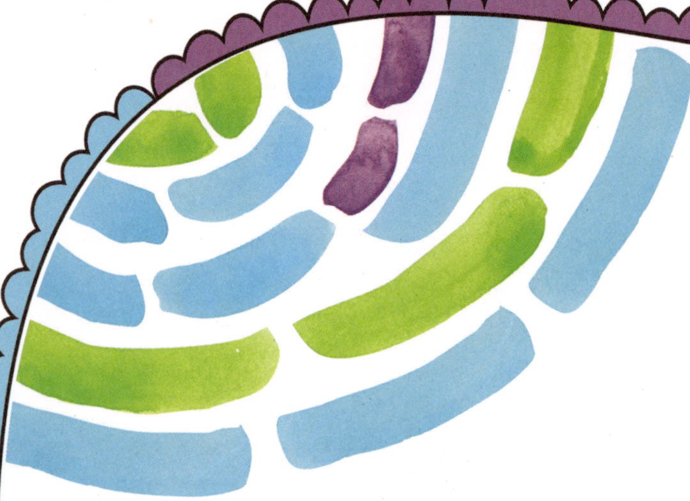

Shapely Ship

Sketcher wants his boat to look more interesting. Fill the sail with shapes and colour them with different colours. You may copy the given pattern.

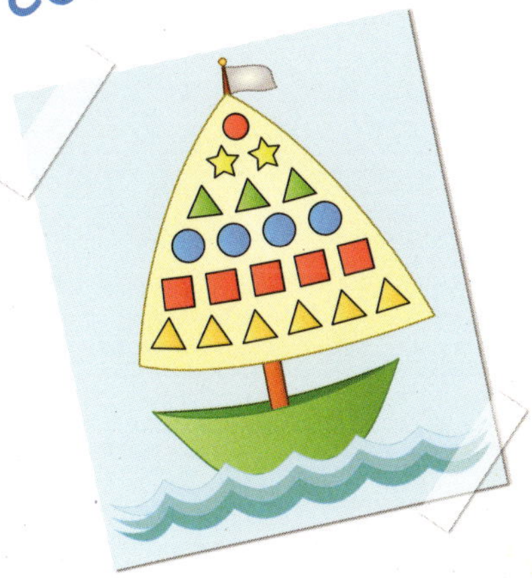

You can draw more waves by making semicircles. You can use different shades of blue.

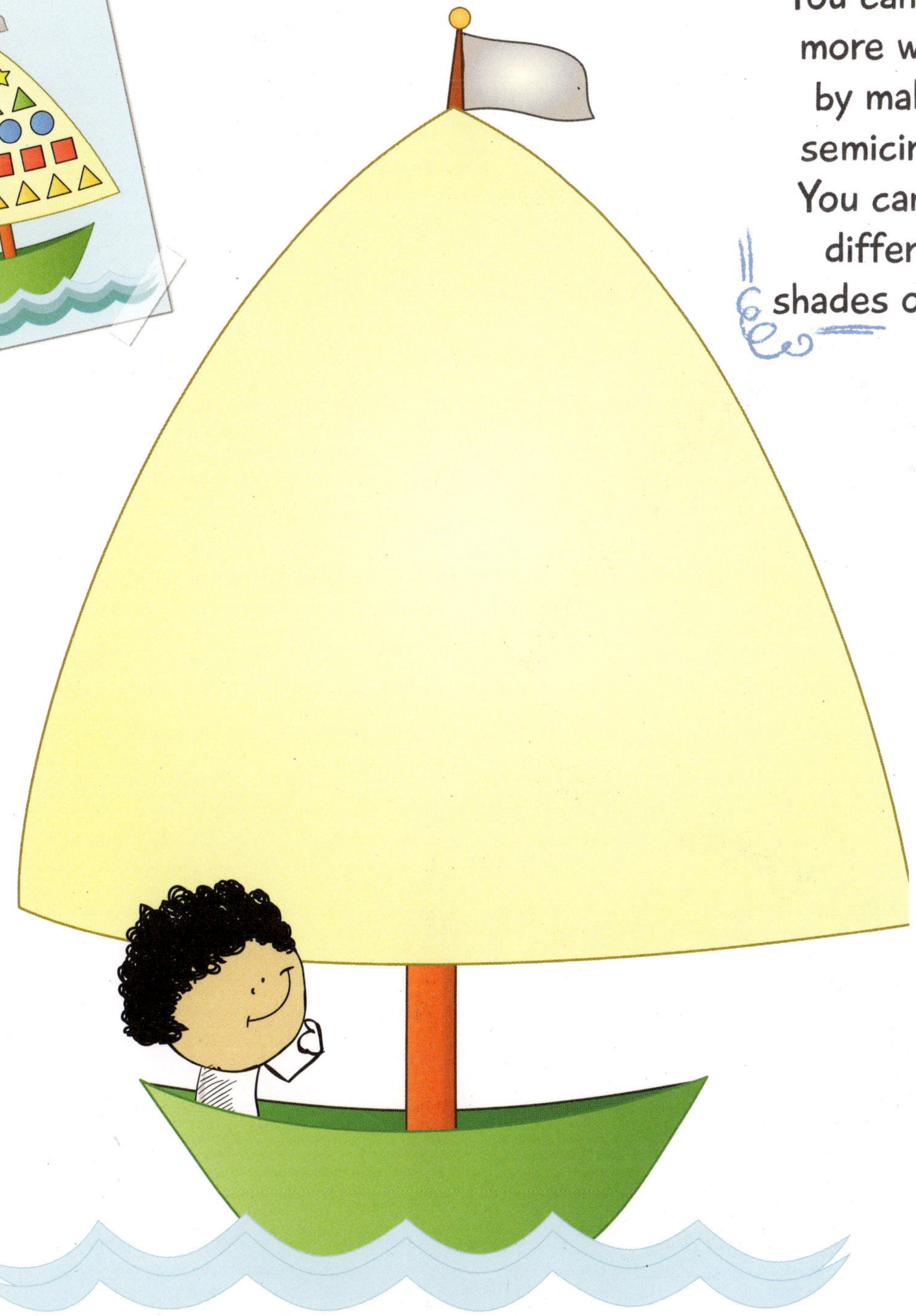

Colourful Food

Help Painter finish this colour wheel using the same colour as the outline.

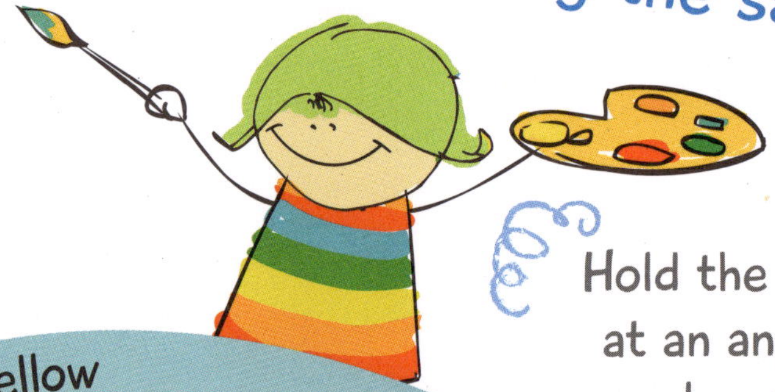

Hold the crayon at an angle to make zigzag lines.

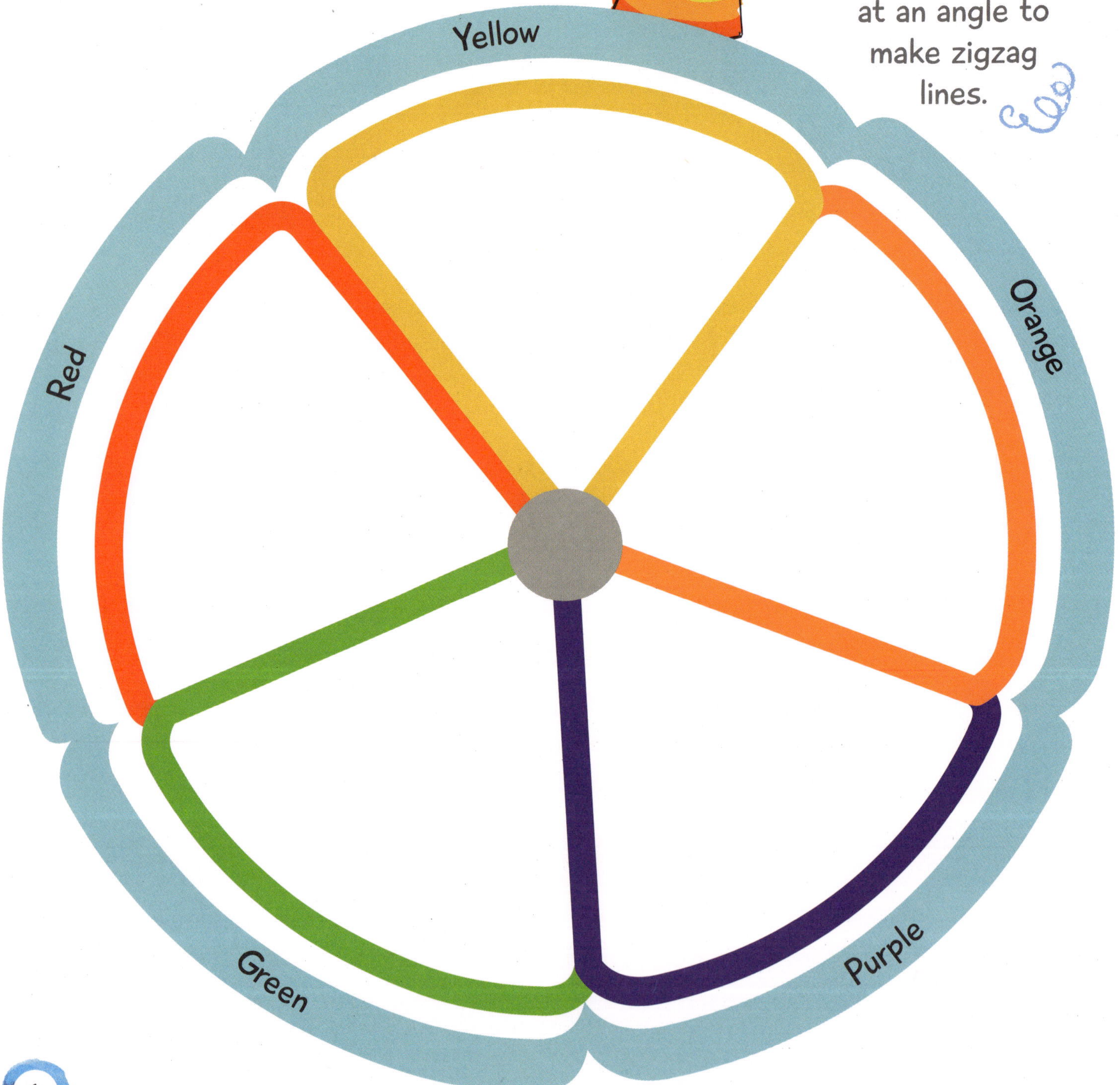

Now, draw and colour a fruit or vegetable for each colour.

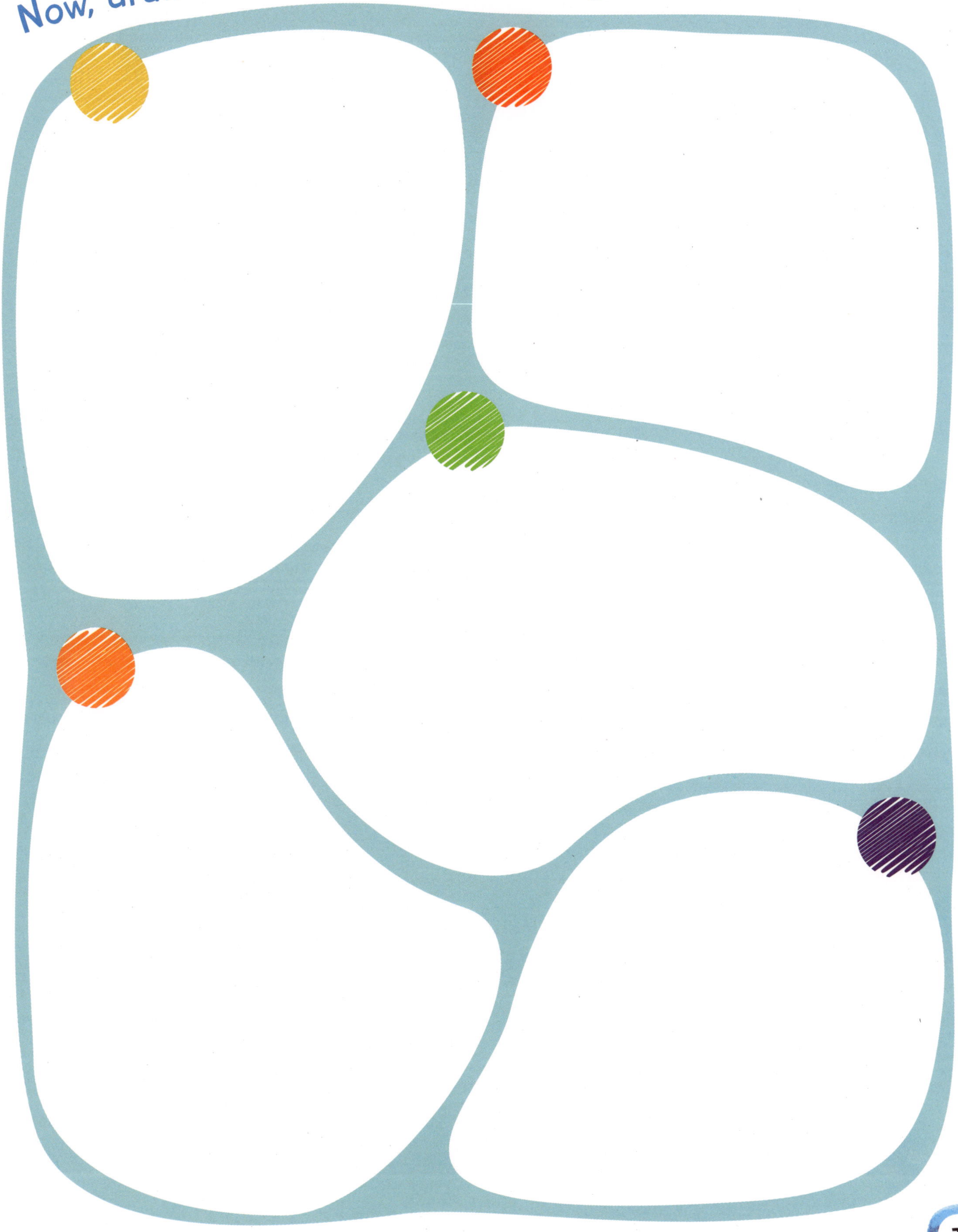

Brushy Bark

Dip an old toothbrush in green paint and spray it in the centre of the page. Hold the book vertically so the extra paint drips downwards, making it look like the bark of a tree.

Hold the toothbrush at a distance from the page. Wash your hands when you're done.

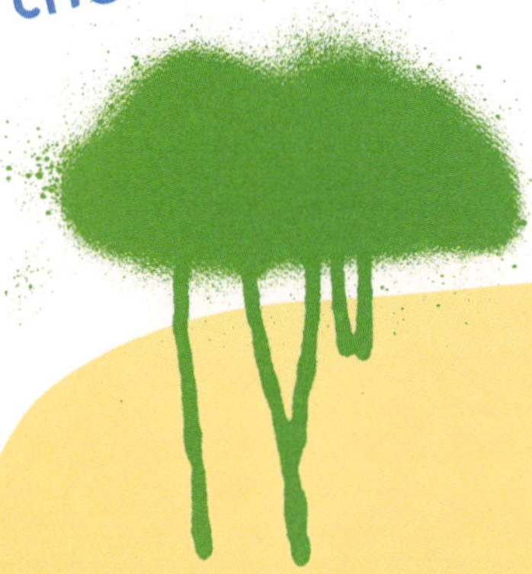

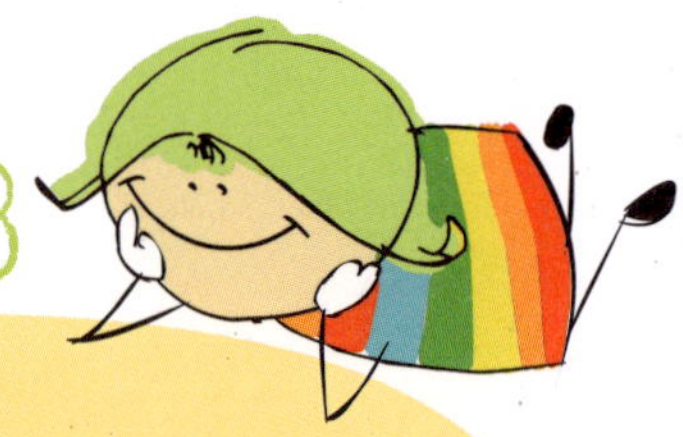

Hand to Glove

Place your hand below and trace its outline. Create a pattern inside and colour it so that it looks like a glove.

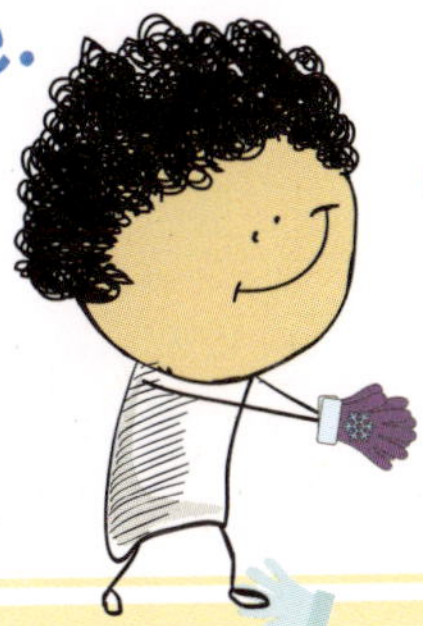

Try drawing outlines of different things in your book.

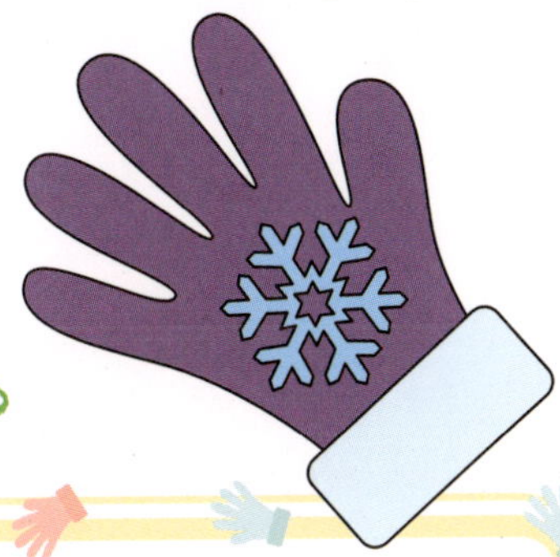

Slow and Steady

Trace over the dotted lines to complete the turtle. Colour the entire picture using crayons.

If you colour slowly, you can stay within the outline.

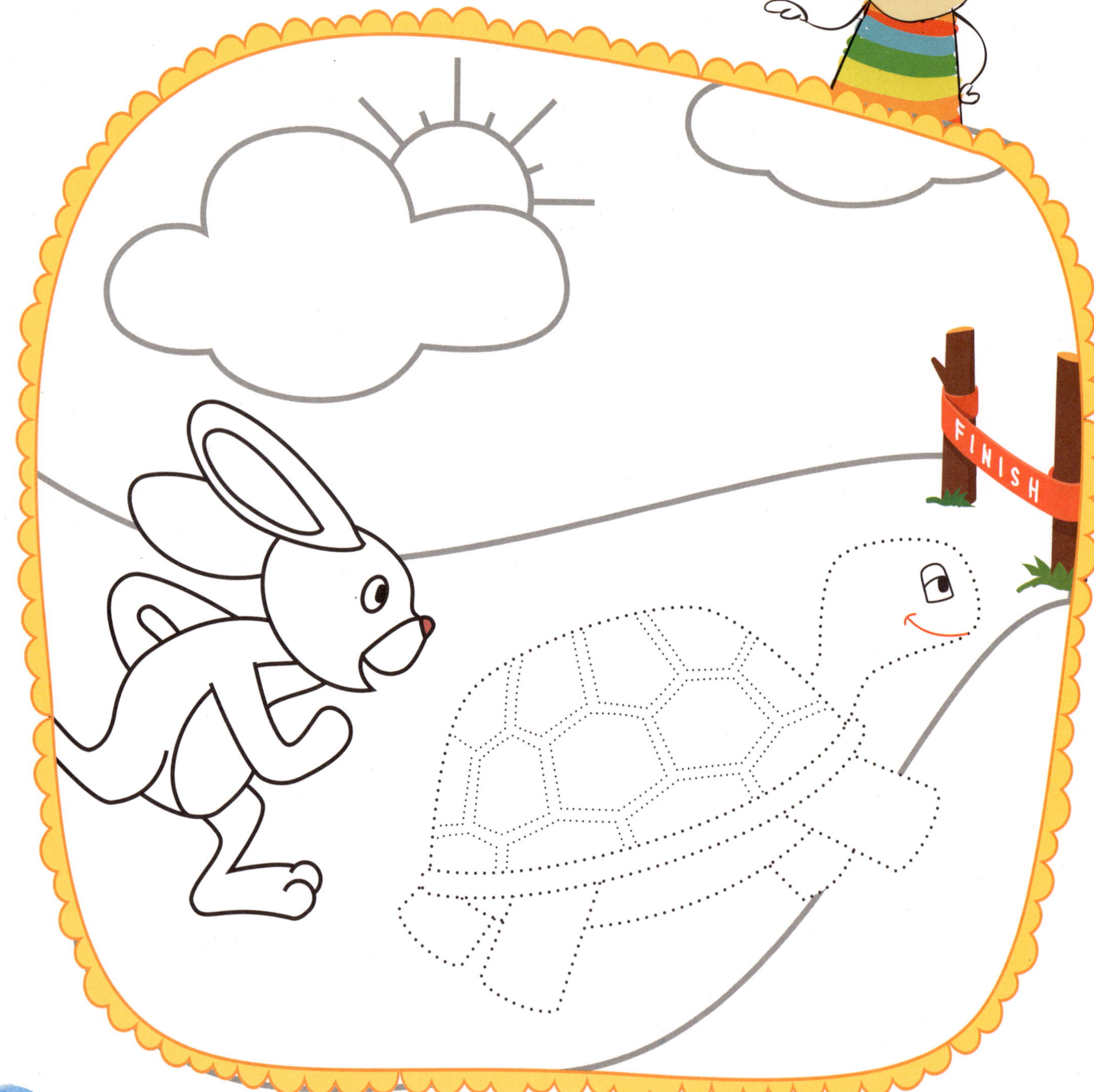

Paint Letters

Ask an adult to cut an ice cream stick in a slanting manner. Dip the cut side in different coloured paints and write the letters of the alphabet. You can also use a twig or a flat brush.

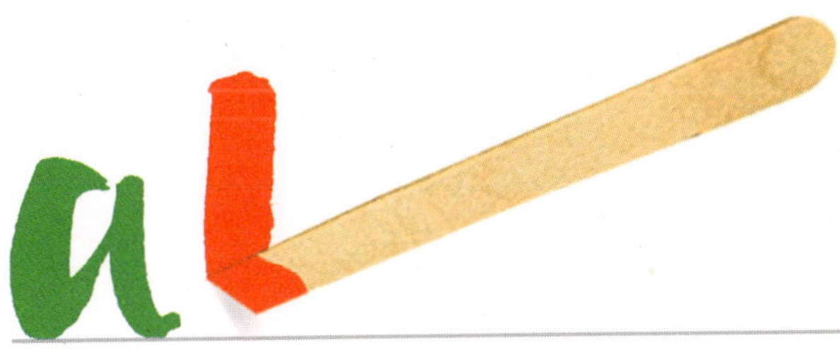

Three-Step Ellie

You can draw Ellie the Elephant in three simple steps! Just follow the steps given below.

1

2

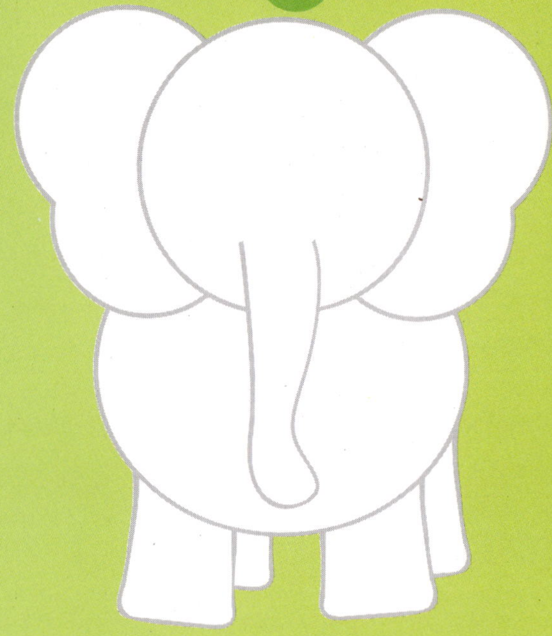

3

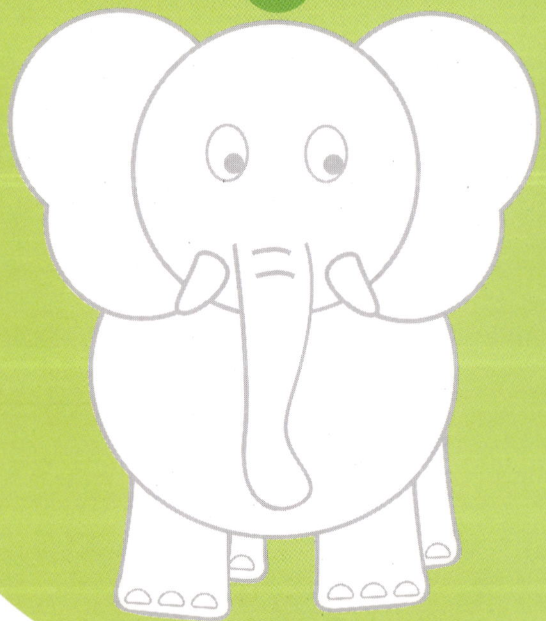

Trace over the steps before you draw an elephant on your own.

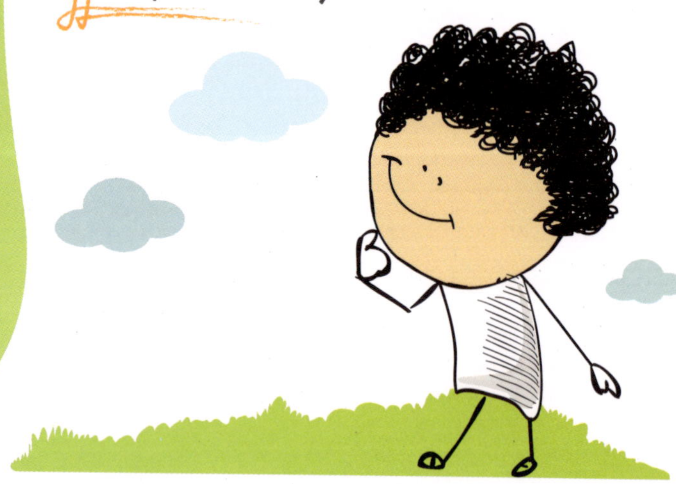

Draw your elephant here. Colour it grey.

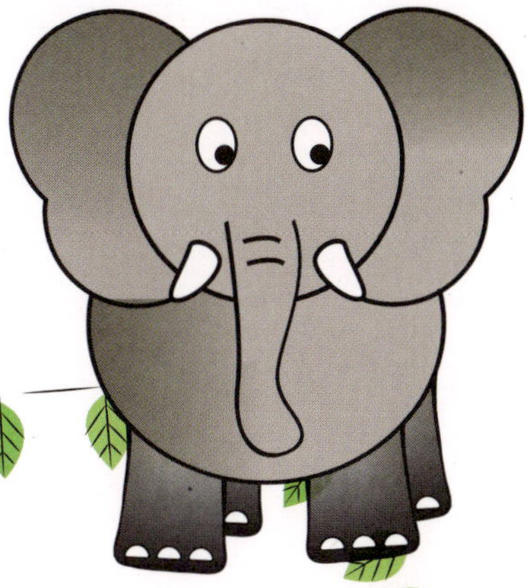

A Stringy Painting

Dip a ball of wool in any paint you like. Roll it in the space below to make a pretty pattern.

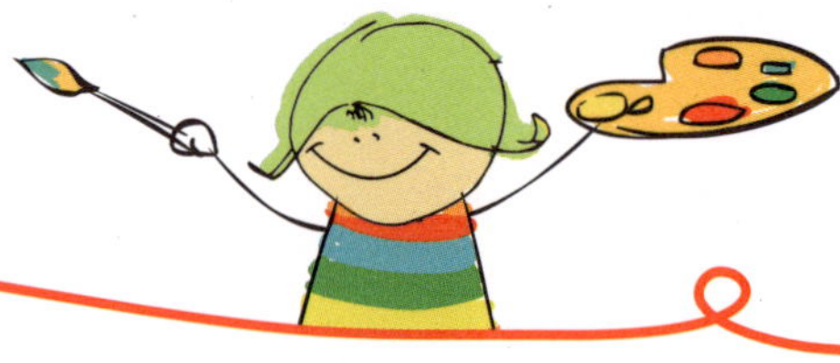

This is a messy activity.
You may need to wear gloves.

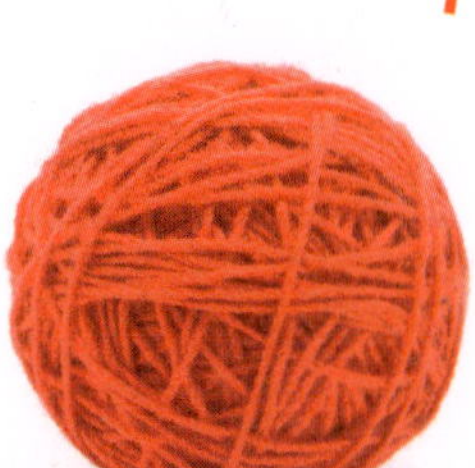

Symmetrical Fun

Follow the grid to draw the other half of the teddy bear. Colour it using crayons.

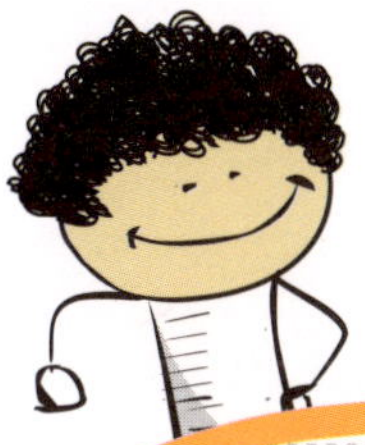

This is a symmetrical picture. Symmetry means that when you fold a picture in the middle, you get the exact same shape on both sides.

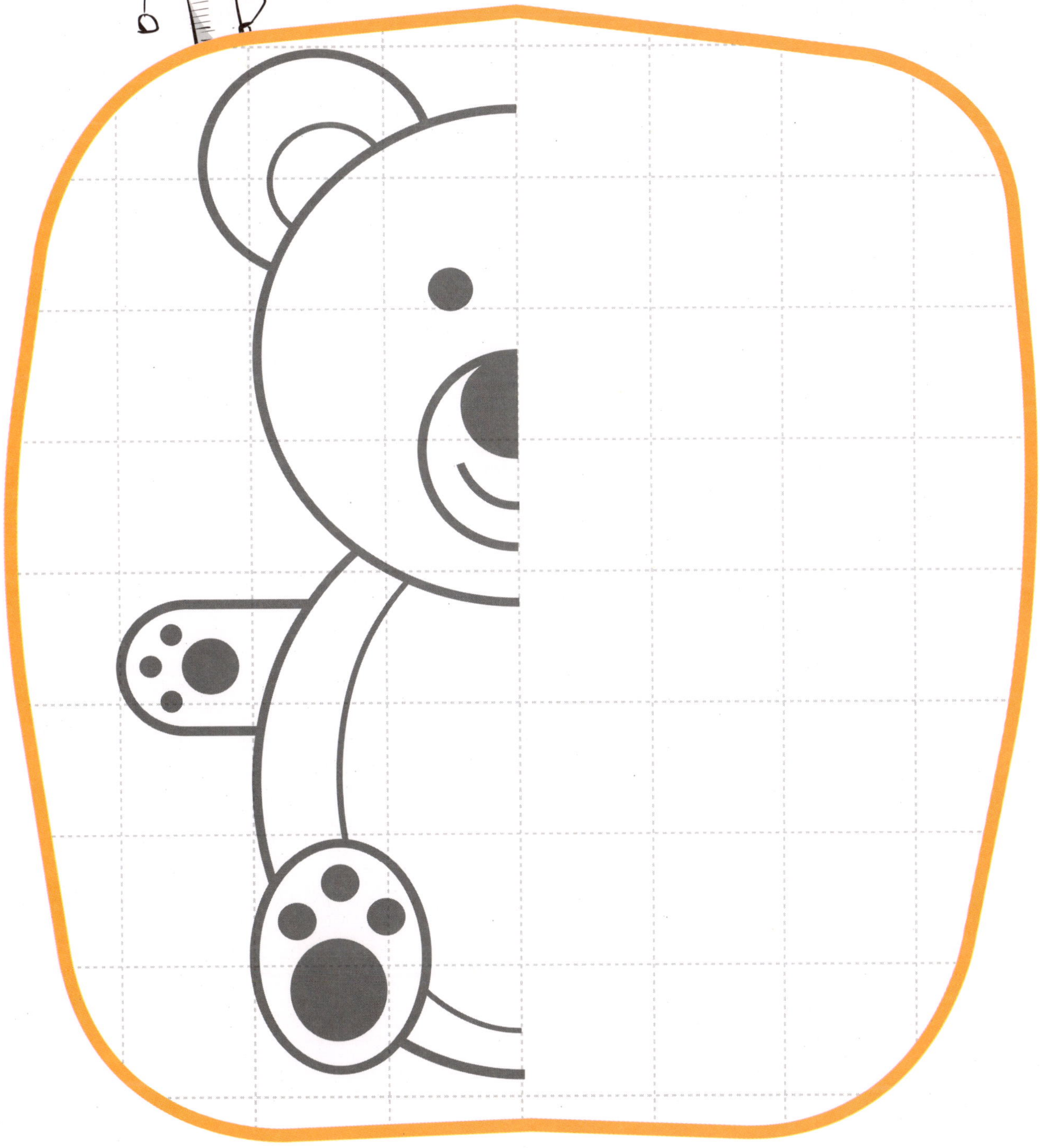

Express Yourself

How many expressions can you think of? Draw them all on the faces given below.

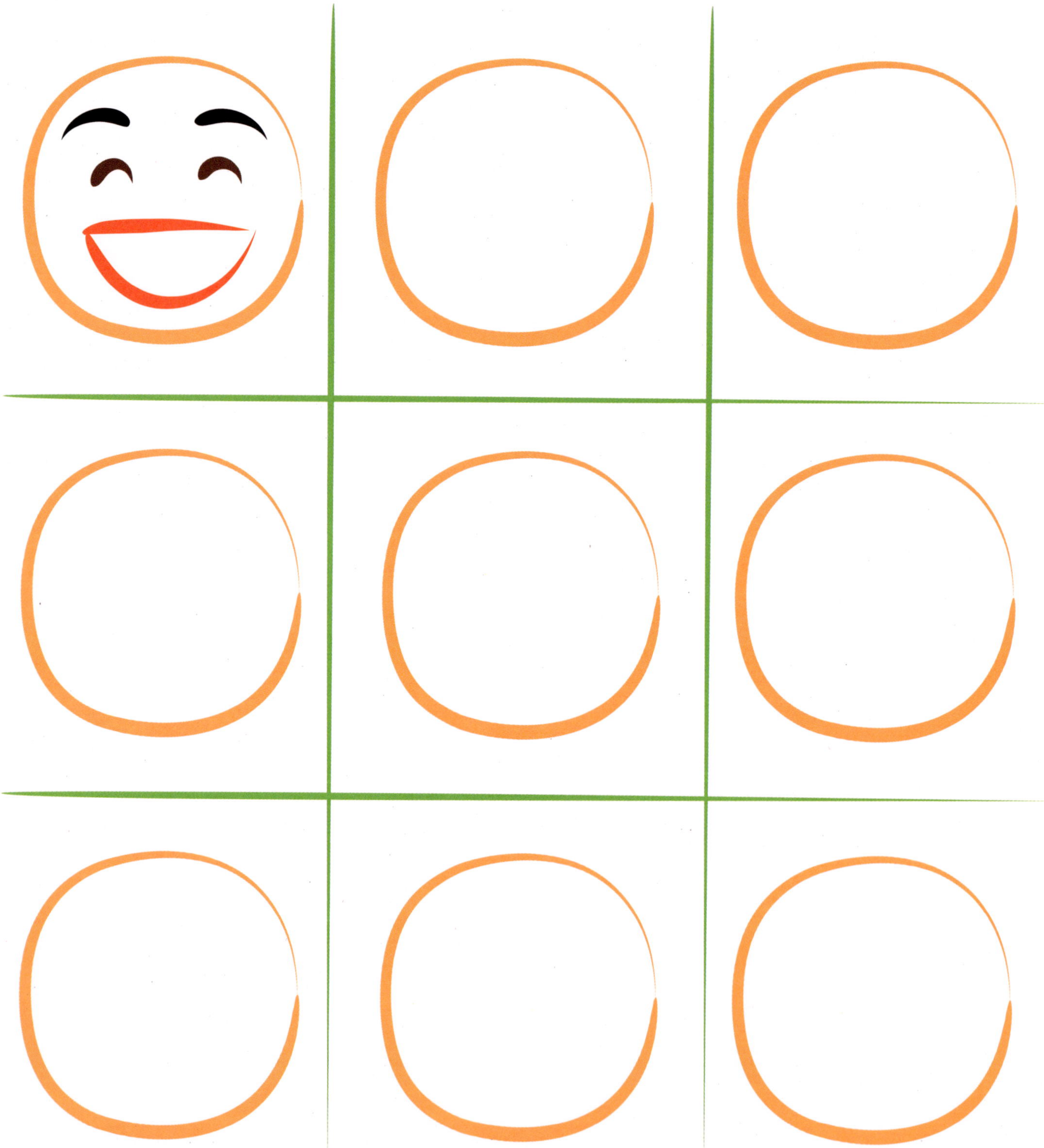

Sponge It!

Dip a sponge in yellow paint and press it within the outlines below. Once the paint dries, draw eyes, beaks and feet to make some chicks!

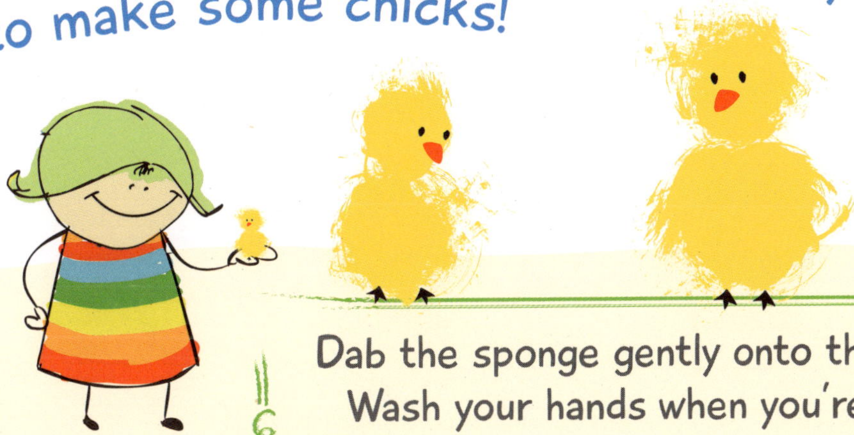

Dab the sponge gently onto the paper.
Wash your hands when you're done.

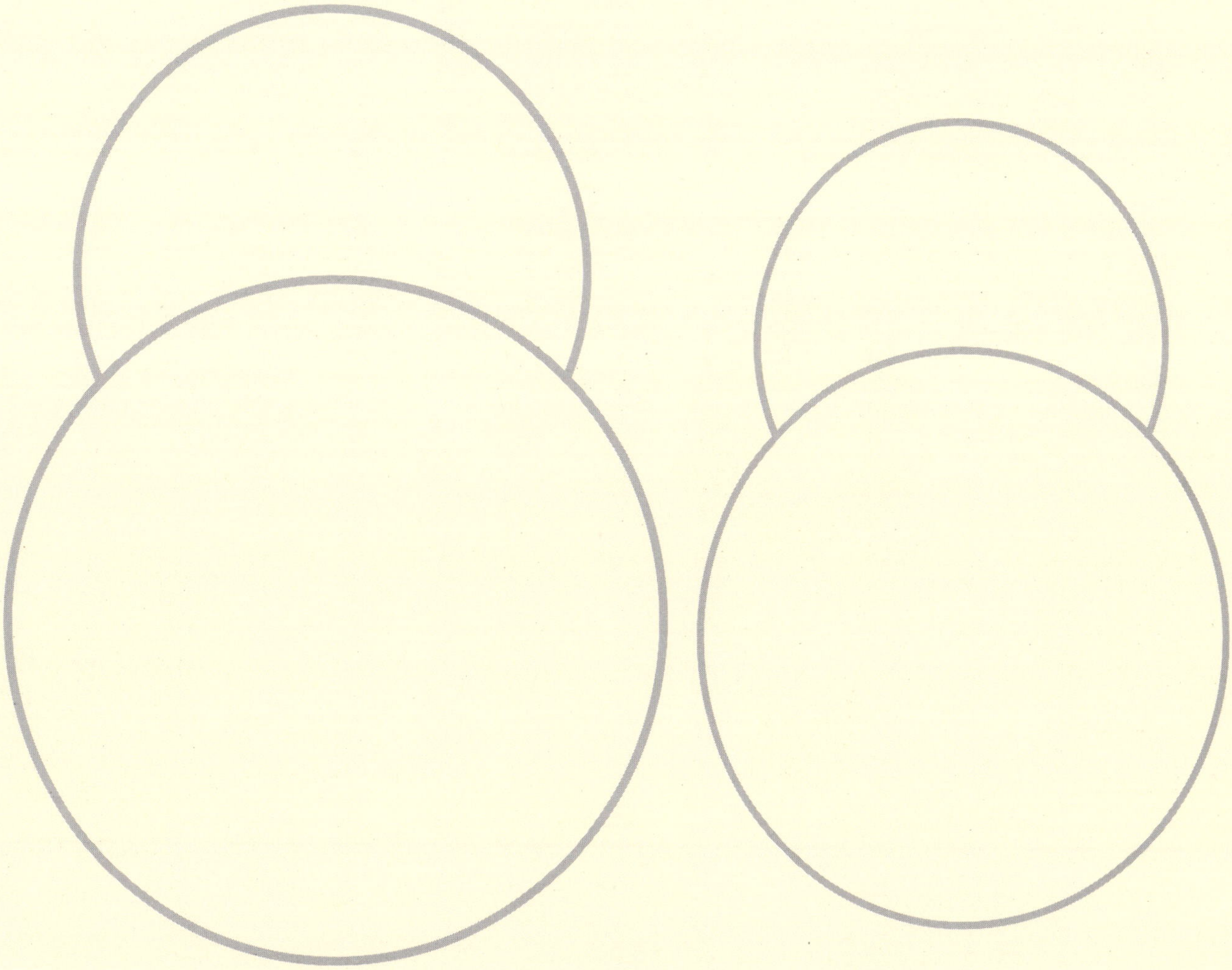

Floral Fun

Do you like flowers? Learn how to draw them in six simple steps. Look at the steps shown below and get started.

1

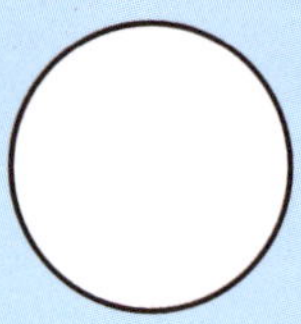

2

3

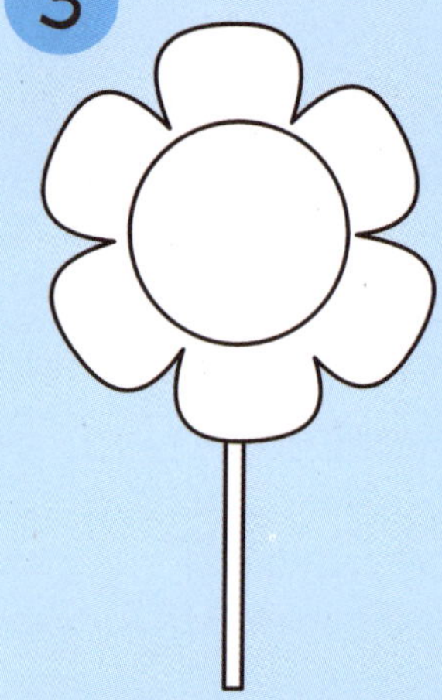

4

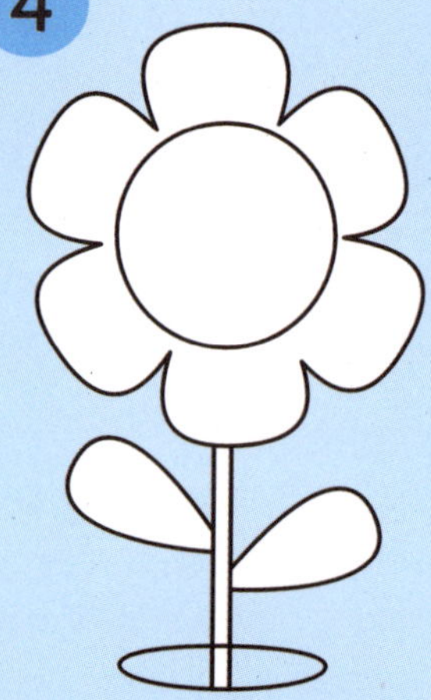

5

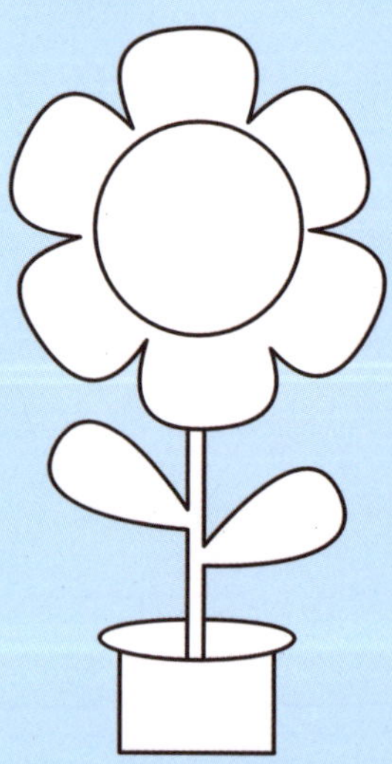

6

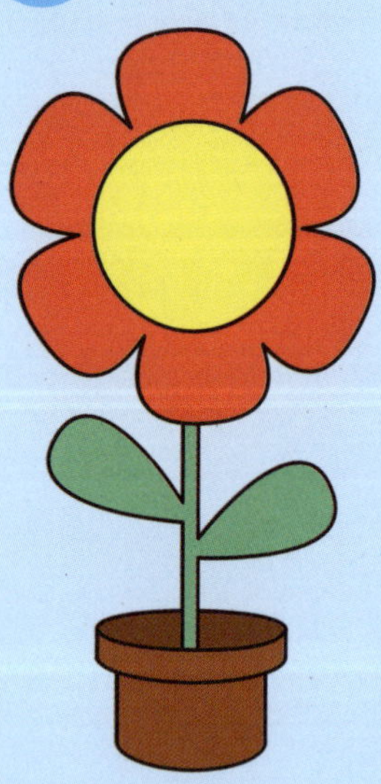

Press the pencil gently on the paper while drawing. This will help you erase the unwanted lines easily.

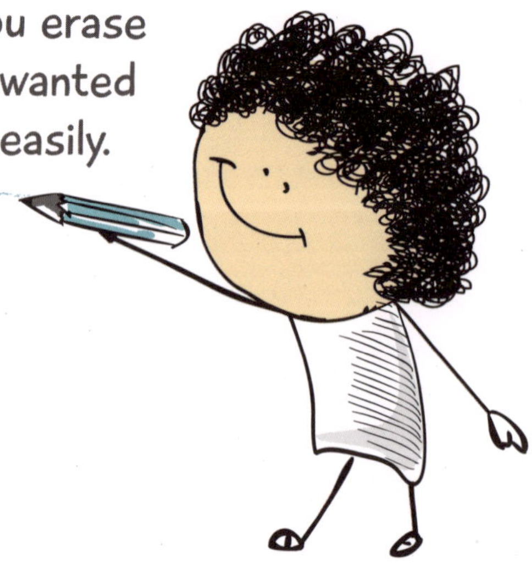

You can draw your flower here.

Crayon and Cream

Painter wants to eat some ice cream. Use different coloured crayons to draw a few ice creams below. Try to make different flavours for her!

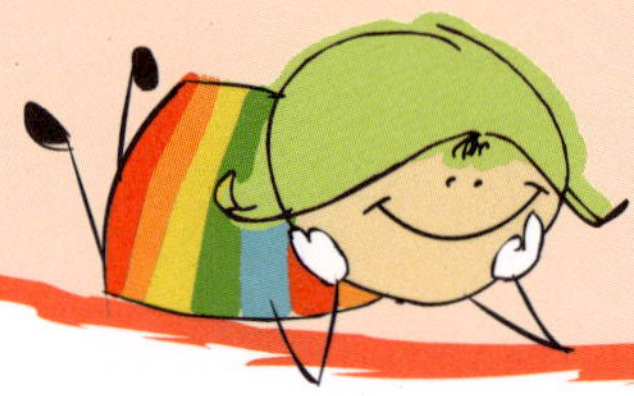

Make it as colourful as you can.

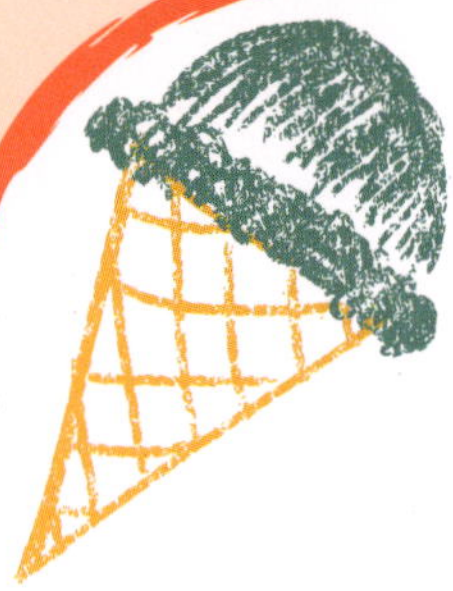

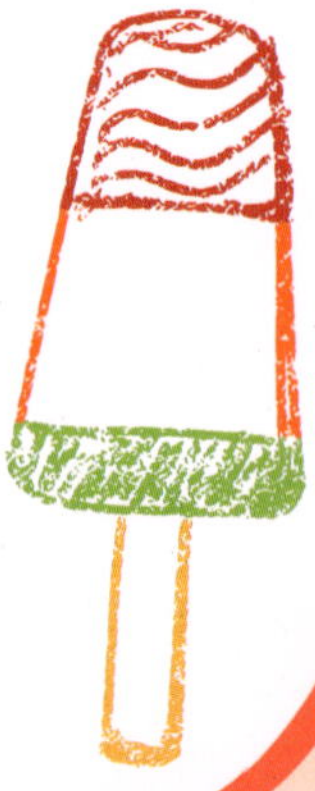

Go Fish!

Follow these five simple steps to draw a fish.

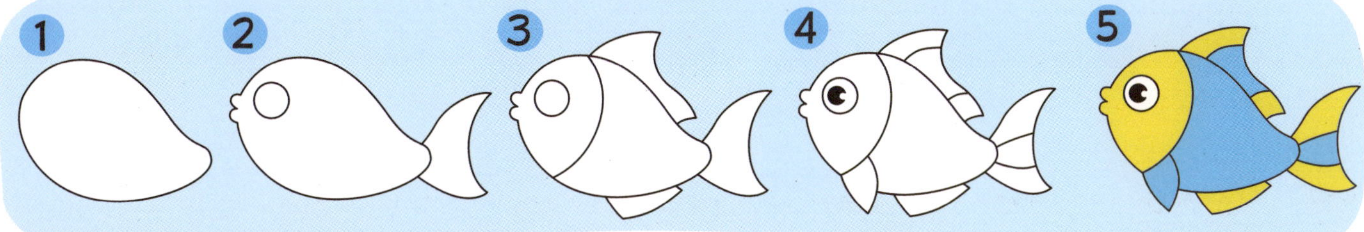

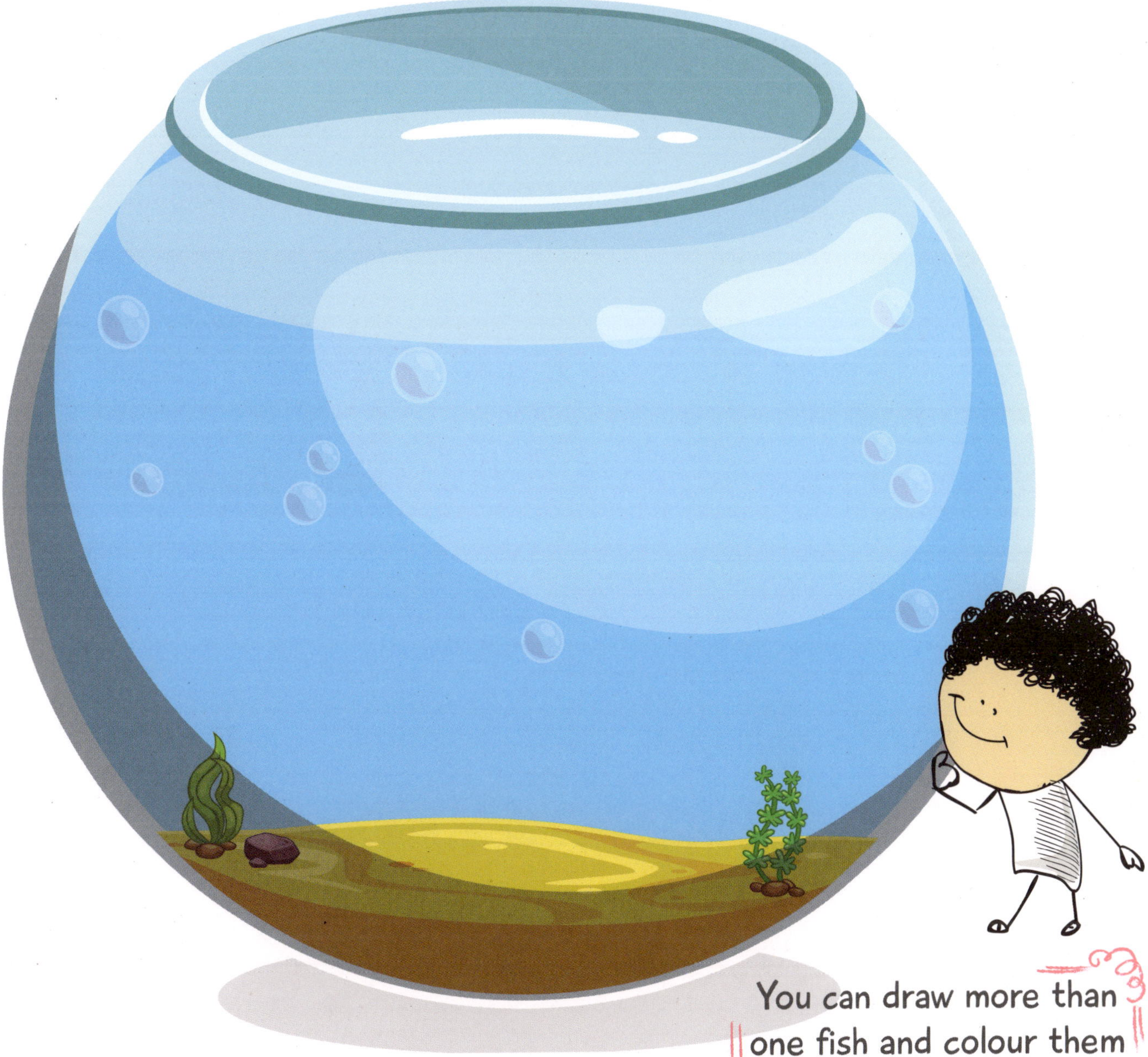

You can draw more than one fish and colour them in different colours.

Colourful Scribbles

Look at the colourful scribbles. Create more scribbles in the columns. Mix different colours to make a pattern in the space given below.

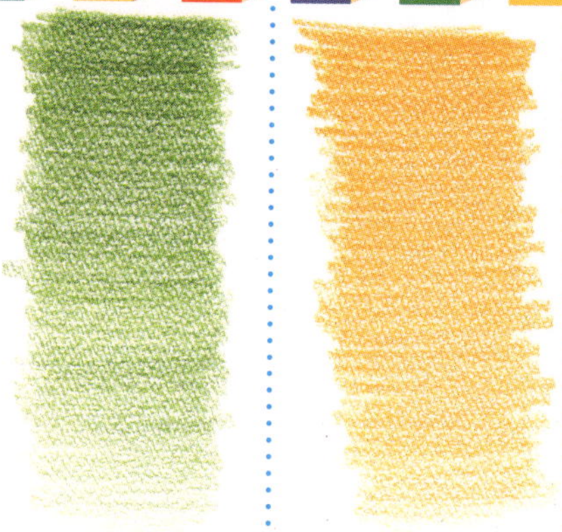

Start with a darker colour such as red.
Colour over it with orange, then yellow.

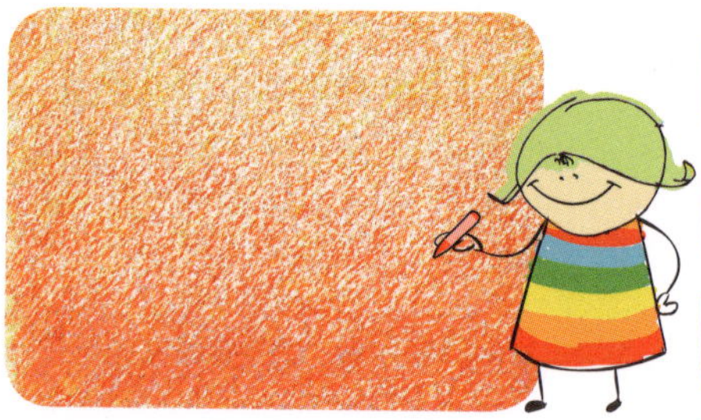

Mystery Mouse

Trace over the dotted lines to complete the drawing.
Colour the picture neatly.

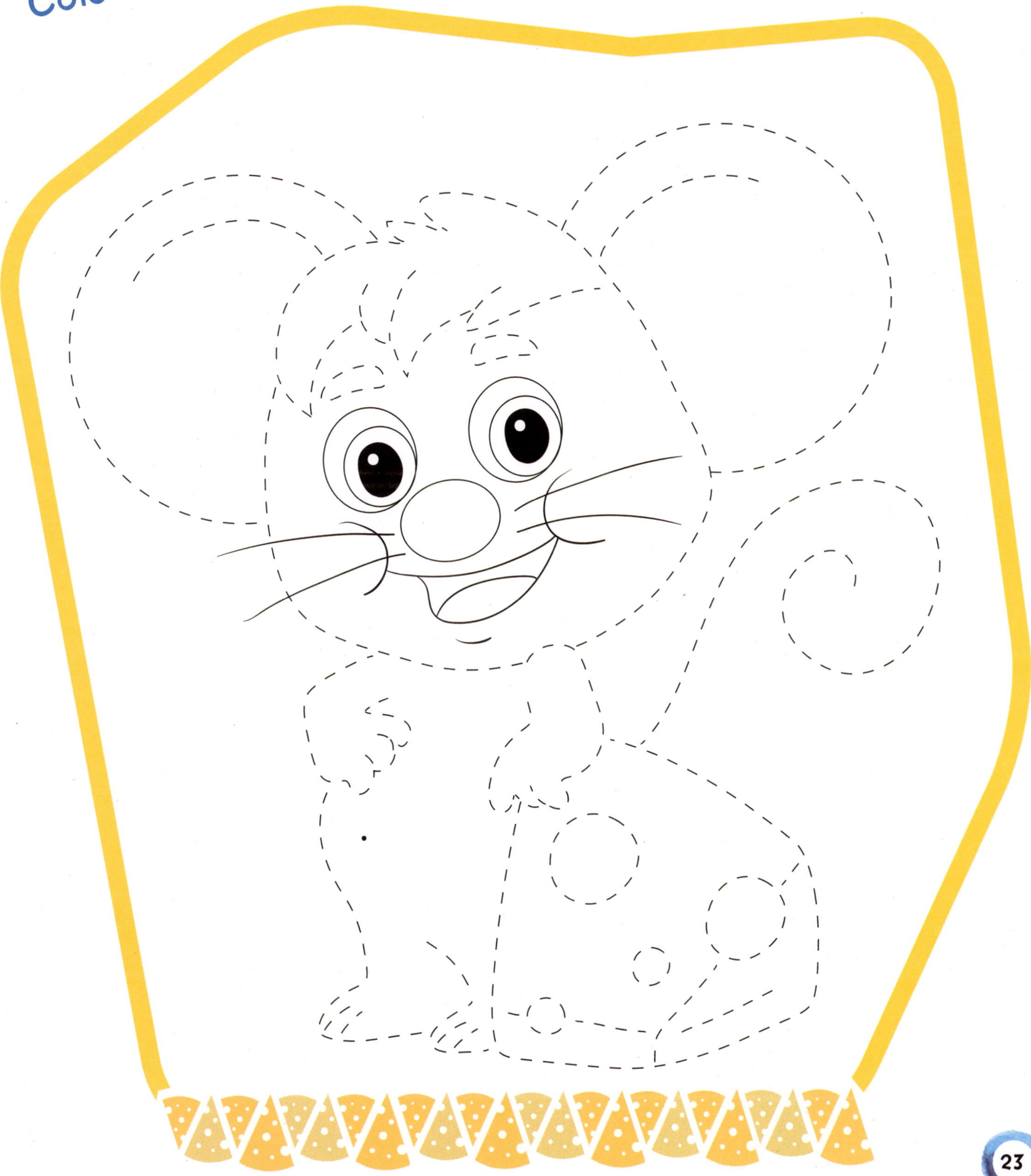

Name Game

Write your name in the space given below. Press colourful dots over it using a cotton bud.

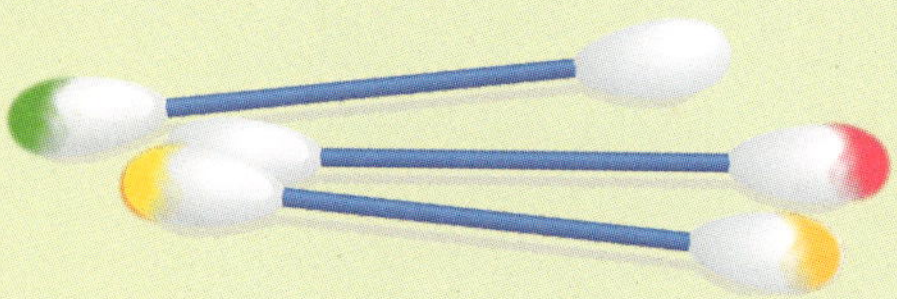

Dip the cotton bud in two different colours to create a special effect.

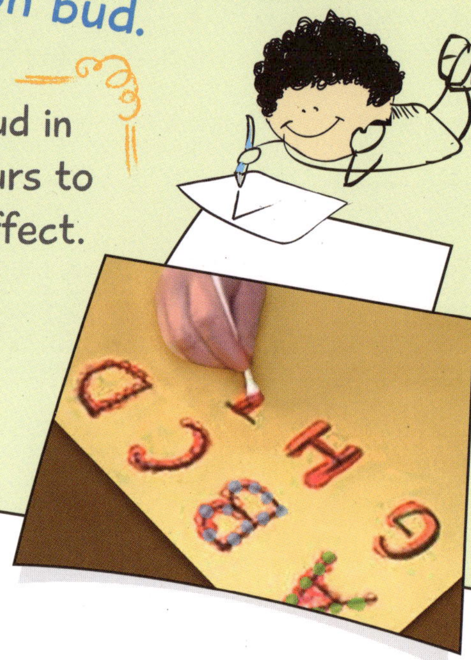

Butterfly Buddy

Painter has to decorate the wings of this butterfly using paint and cotton buds. Can you help her?

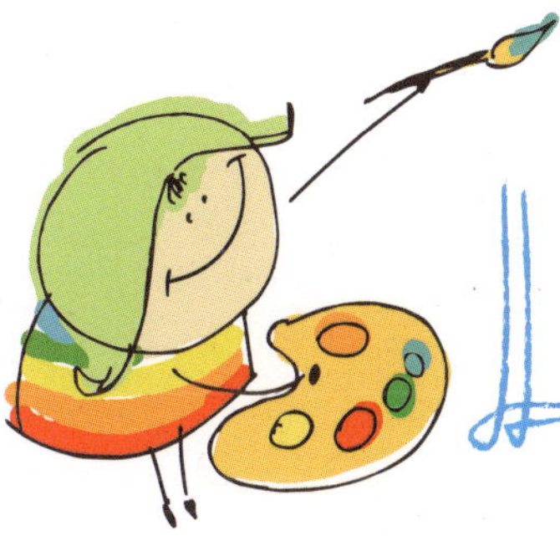

Dip cotton buds in different colours to make your butterfly colourful.

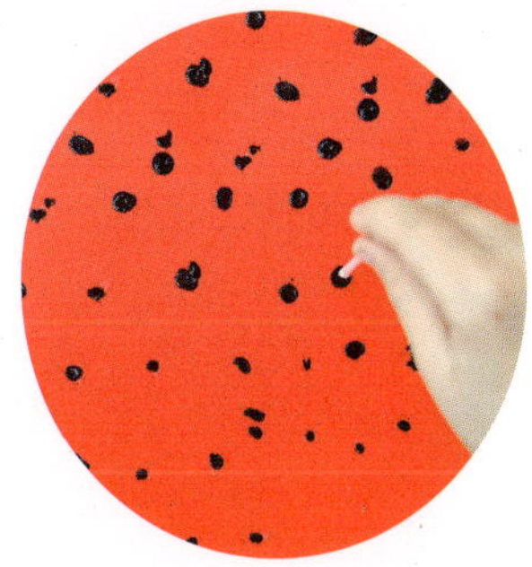

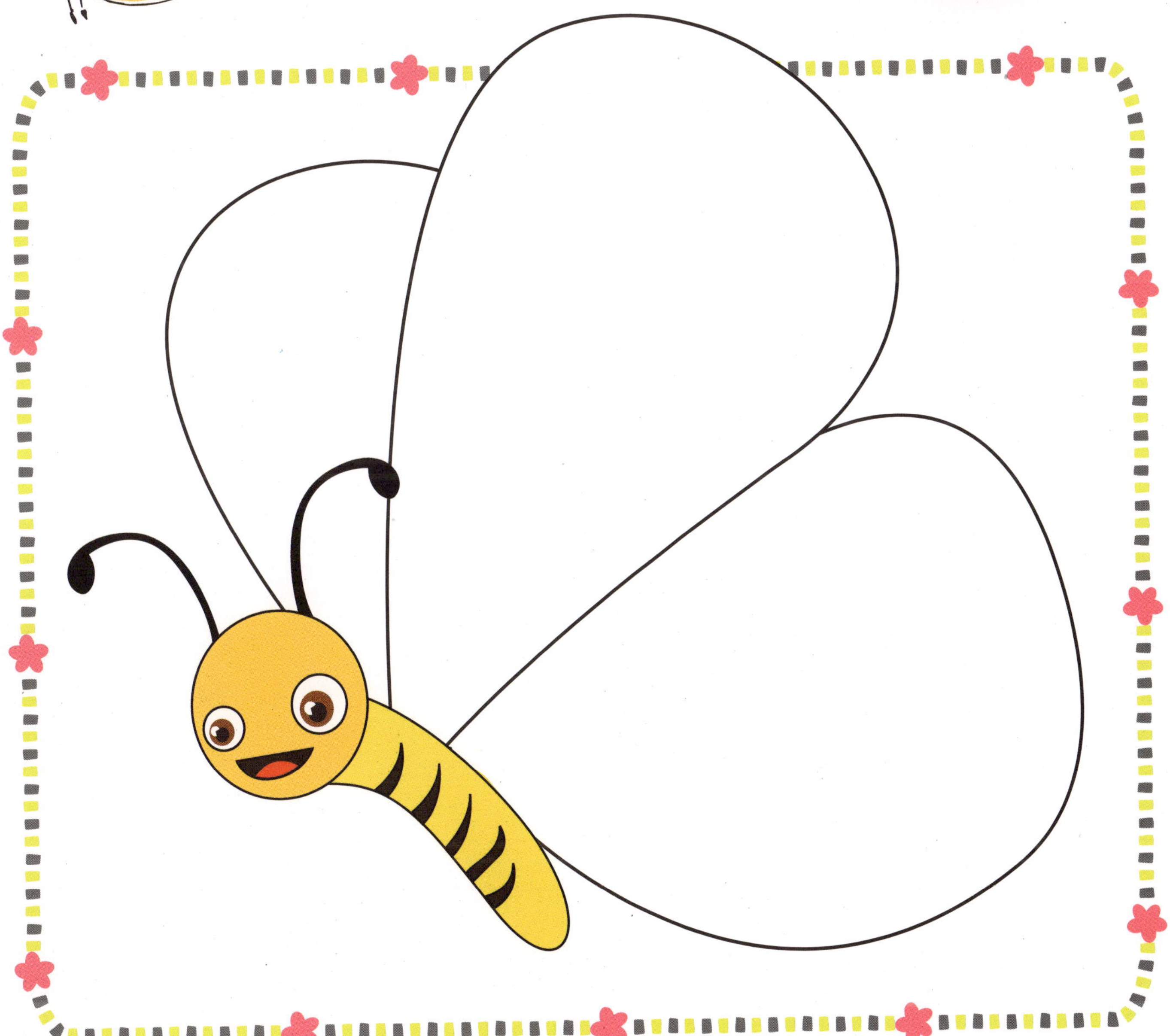

Warli Painting

Use a white colour pencil to trace over these stick figures. Then, create your own stick figure painting in the space given below. This form of art is called Warli painting.

Beautiful City

Painter wants to make a pretty city painting. Help her by adding people, trees, clouds and more on the canvas below.

Draw with a black pencil first. Then, colour the whole thing neatly.

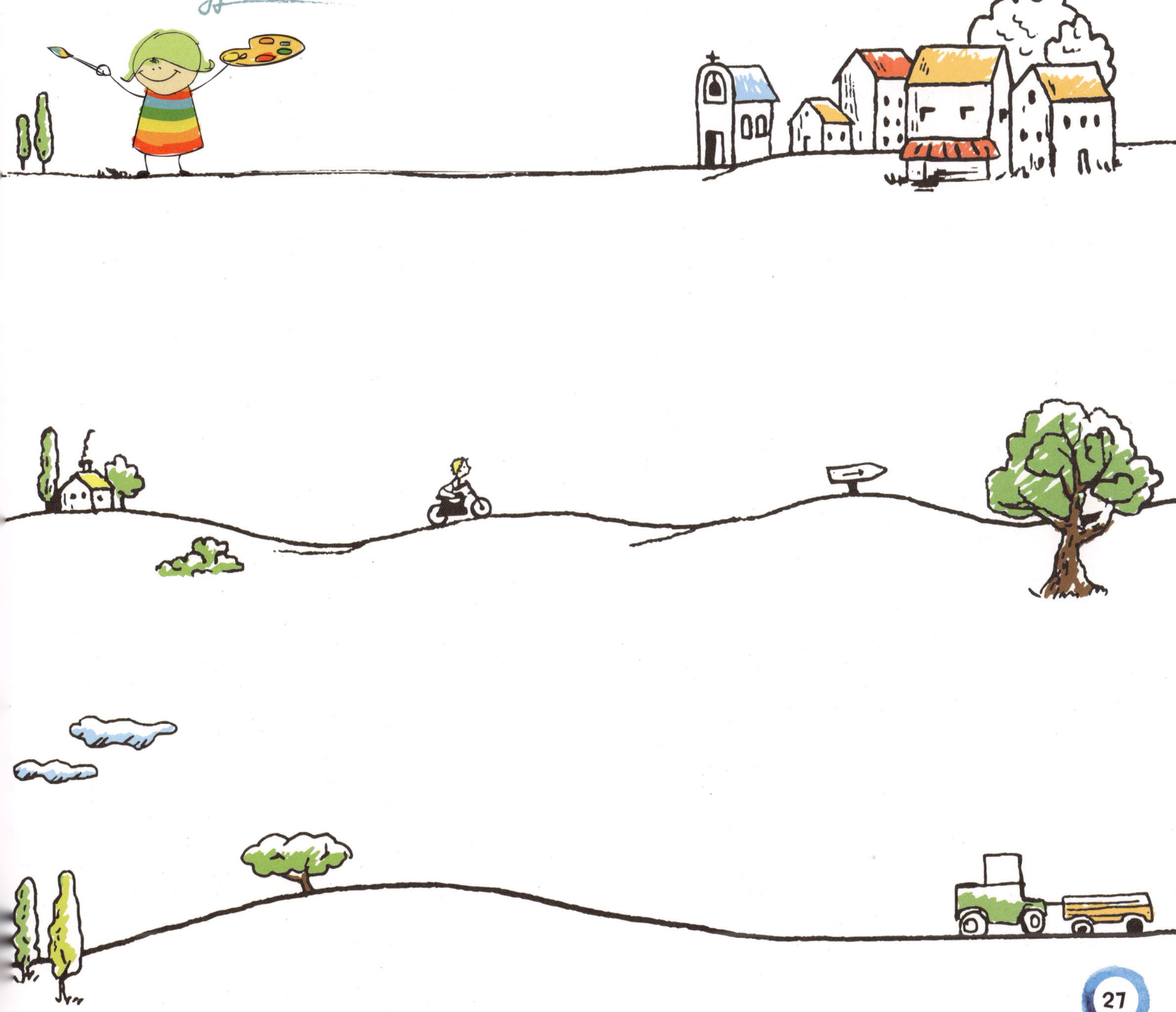

Sticky Sport

Copy these stick figures in the boxes alongside.

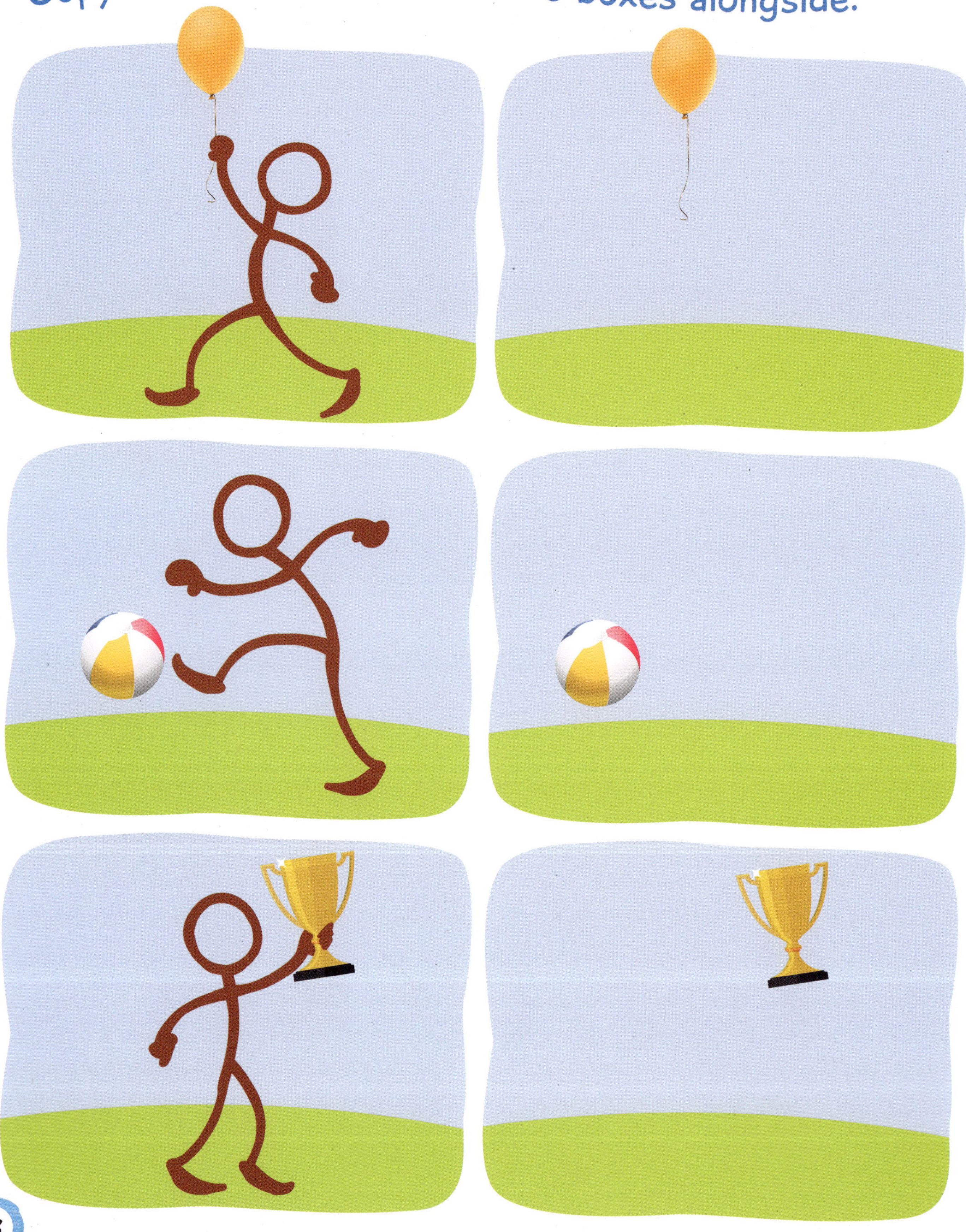

Popping Circle

Draw a circle in the space below. Draw sleeping lines all around it. Within the circle, draw curves and join the sleeping lines outside. That will make the circle pop!

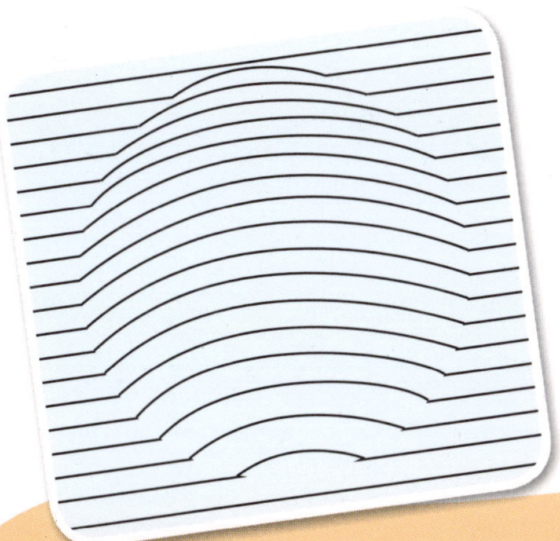

Trace the circle lightly so that it is not visible when you finish making your optical illusion.

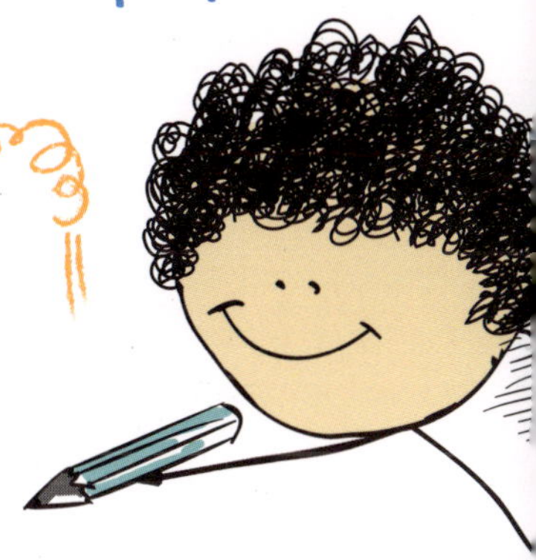

Designer Bracelets

Draw different designs on the bracelet outlines below!

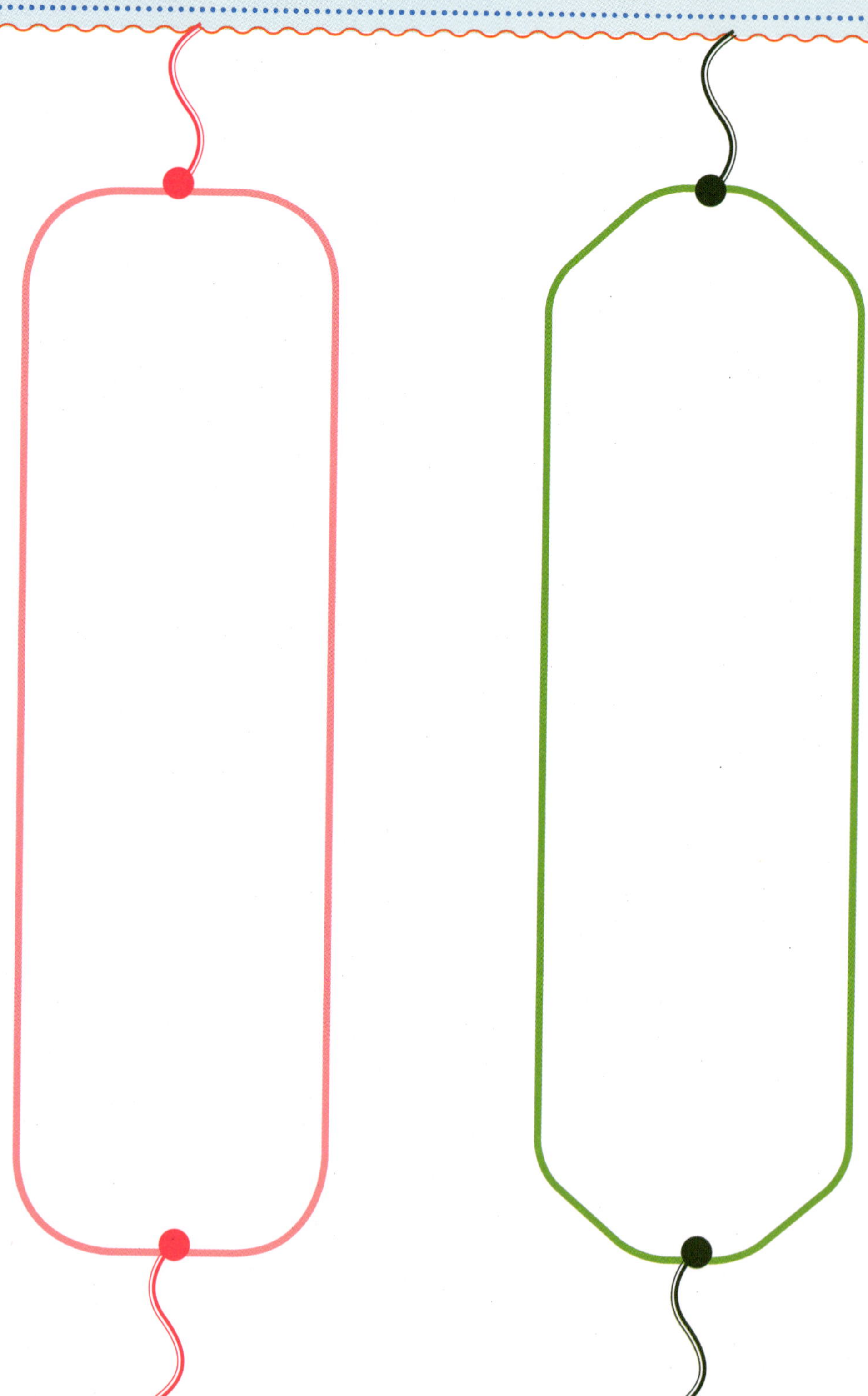

Sock Puppets

Put up a puppet show! Colour these sock puppets pretty and bright! Add a joke as a dialogue that's fun and light!

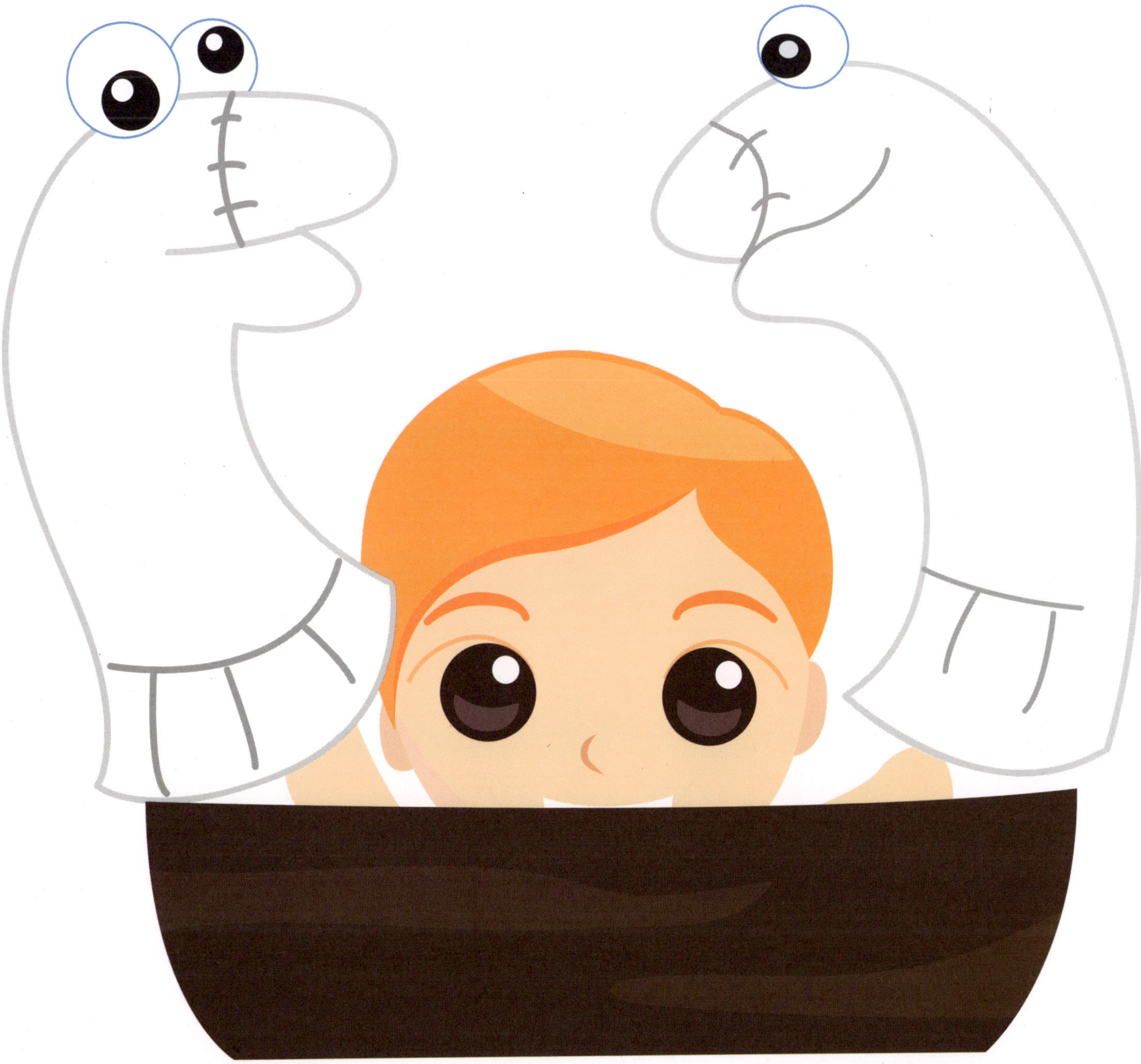

Hide and Seek

Colour the blocks with a dot to spot the hidden animal.

Use two colours, one for the blocks with dots and another for the remaining blocks.

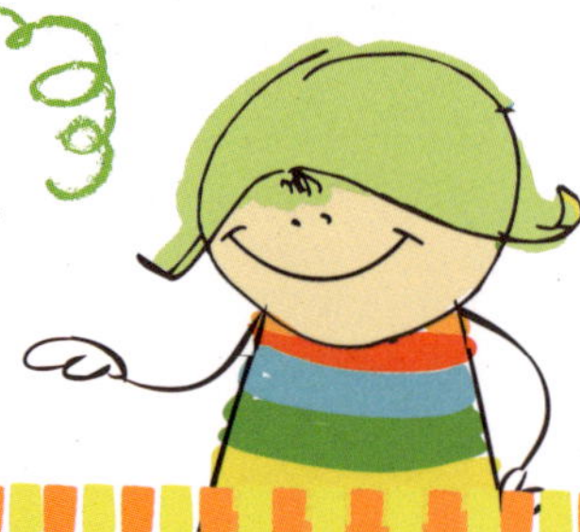

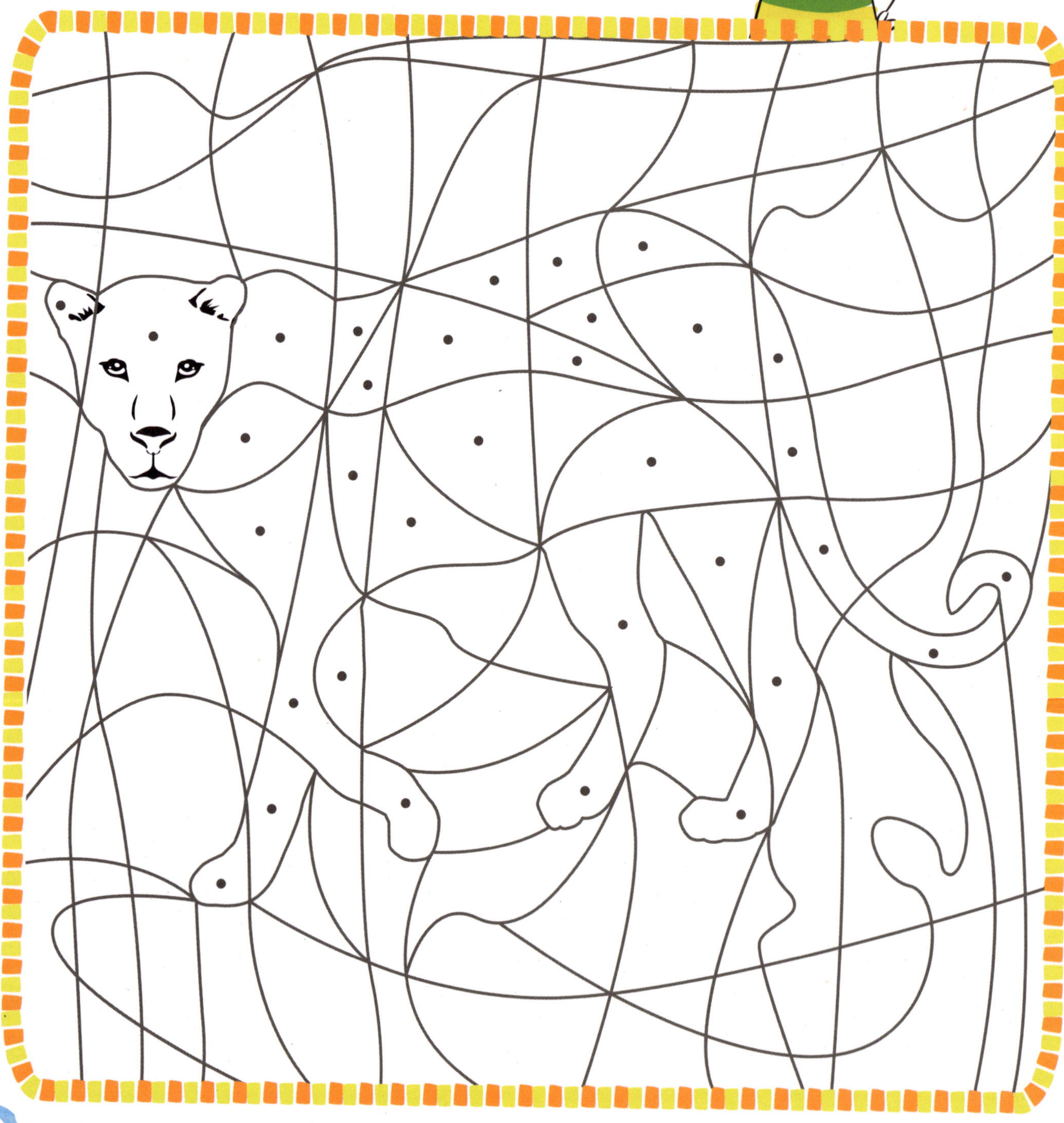